MUMKIN

Written By
STEPHEN COSGROVE

Illustrated By
ROBIN JAMES

Rourke Enterprises, Inc.
Vero Beach, FL 32964

A Serendipity™ Book

© 1986 Rourke Enterprises, Inc.
© 1986 Price/Stern/Sloan Publishers, Inc.

Library of Congress Cataloging in Publication Data

Cosgrove, Stephen.
  Mumkin.

  "A Serendipity book."
  Summary: Hating to share, Mumkin the pony builds
a high fence around his part of the meadow but finds
himself a prisoner when the other ponies build
similar fences.
  [1. Sharing—Fiction.   2. Ponies—Fiction.
3. Conduct of life—Fiction]   I. James, Robin, ill.
II. Title.
PZ7.C8187Mv 1986   [Fic]   86-15635
ISBN 0-86592-242-X

Dedicated to two great men. Together one day in Geneva they tried to see a world without borders of thicket and vine.

Stephen

The morning mists swirled and twirled in the hesitant breeze that always blew just after the sun had risen. They twisted in and about the gnarled old trees and stumps that surrounded the rippling grasses, that seemed as a sea when the winds did blow. This place was called Middling Meadow.

Middling Meadow was a wide and spacious land with natural borders of cedar and pine, meadow and mountain, and a twisty, little stream.

In Middling Meadow lived a herd of small horses who roamed freely from one side of the meadow to the other as they pranced and galloped about. For the land was open, and all the horses shared in all there was to share, from the sweet-tasting clover down by the stream, to the honeysuckle vine that grew in great profusion in and around the aspen pine.

Living in this herd of horses was a pudgy little pony called Mumkin, who lived to eat all that he could of the clover and honeysuckle vine. His flaxen mane rippled and flowed as he ran about the meadow in search of good things to eat. When he had eaten all that he could, he would drink deeply of the cold, sweet waters of the bubbling brook, and then stand in silent slumber in a streaming ray of sunshine.

Mumkin felt that he knew where every succulent blade of grass grew in the meadow, and he was not about to share that with any of the other horses. Whenever he was eating and another pony approached, he would lower his head, flatten his ears and squint his eyes to scare it away. The other ponies usually squinted right back, unafraid, and meandered off to munch another bunch of clover or honeysuckle vine.

Mumkin hated sharing so much that he finally decided to do something about it. With his strong teeth, he began to drag sticks and twigs, branches and boughs from the forest. Pulling and tugging, he built a border of thicket and vine around what he felt was the most luscious part of the pasture.

He built his border higher and higher until none of the other ponies could even look in. Then at either end he built gates that only he could enter. Mumkin paced his border, shaking his shaggy mane from side to side in great delight. Now, no other pony would be able to eat his luscious grasses! No other pony would be able to munch his sweet honeysuckle vine. This was his land! His very own part of the pasture! Mumkin was very pleased indeed.

That night, bathed in sparkling starlight and beams from a bright silver moon, he slept in peace and tranquillity. Well, almost slept, for he had to remain alert just in case another pony attempted to cross his border during the night. Though none did, he could hear rustling outside his walls. Mumkin became so worried that he paced all night long, trying to see what was happening beyond his walls — but he could see nothing at all. For you see, the bad thing about borders is that you have to build them so high that you cannot see beyond them.

The next morning Mumkin woke just as the first rays of bright light stabbed their way through his border of thicket and vine. He looked quickly around to be certain no one had entered during the night. Sure enough, Mumkin was all alone. Every blade of grass was safe, and his and his alone. He kicked his heels and reeled about his private land spraying rainbow showers of morning dew. He nibbled a bit of breakfast, then decided it was time to dash to the stream for a drink of water. So, after he made sure that his walls were safe and secure, he slipped through his border gate to go to the creek.

Much to Mumkin's surprise, the pasture of the day before was now nothing but a series of borders of thicket and vine. For, during the night, as he slept in his borders, the other ponies had built walls of their own. Now there was no open space to roam free.

Mumkin wandered around in circles, trying to find the stream, but in this maze he could find nothing but border upon border. He tried over and over to slip through one border or another, but at each there was an angry pony with ears flattened, glaring and warning him back.

Amid the maze of borders Mumkin could not find his own tiny land, and was lost in walls of thicket and vine. 'Round and 'round he ran, then walked between and through the borders until finally he found himself on the narrow trail that reached to the very top of Middling Mountain.

"Certainly," he thought to himelf, "if I get high enough I will be able to spy my own borders." But no matter where he looked he could see, nothing that looked familiar. Finally, he climbed to the very top of the mountain, to the place where even clouds refused to go. Here he stopped to rest, for he was very, very tired.

Mumkin looked down at all there was to see. He looked once, twice and then again, for from this great height he could see none of the borders that he and the other ponies had built. As far as he could see, there was only the Middling Meadow as it had been created — without walls, without borders. He stood there, looking for a long, long while until the tears of regret for what he had done dripped slowly from the corners of his eyes.

"What a fool I've been!" he said as he reared in anger. "We must all share this meadow together!" And he raced down the steep rock path with his flaxen mane snapping like a whip in the wind.

Tears streaming down his face, Mumkin tore at his border of thicket and vine, scattering his walls into the wind. When the other ponies saw what he was doing, they too began to destroy the evil that they had created. Middling Meadow returned to the way it had been intended to be.

Well, almost as it had been intended, for one grey, greedy mare had left up her border walls. She continued to peer out nervously, afraid that someone might sneak into her section of the meadow. And there she stayed as the others played, trapped by the fear of losing what she thought belonged to her alone.

TEAR DOWN YOUR BORDERS
OF THICKET AND VINE
CREATING A FREE WORLD,
YOURS AND MINE